I love you

CARLE

Rooster Is Off to See the World

by Eric Carle

READY-TO-READ

SIMON SPOTLIGHT

New York   London   Toronto   Sydney   New Delhi

This book was previously published with slightly different text as *Rooster's Off to See the World*.

SIMON SPOTLIGHT

An imprint of Simon & Schuster Children's Publishing Division

1230 Avenue of the Americas, New York, New York 10020

Copyright © 1972 by Eric Carle Corp.

Eric Carle's name and signature logo type are registered trademarks of Eric Carle.

First Simon Spotlight Ready-to-Read edition 2013

For information about special discounts for bulk purchases, please contact Simon & Schuster Special Sales at 1-866-506-1949 or business@simonandschuster.com.

The Simon & Schuster Speakers Bureau can bring authors to your live event. For more information or to book an event contact the Simon & Schuster Speakers Bureau at 1-866-248-3049 or visit our website at www.simonspeakers.com.

Manufactured in the United States of America 0313 LAK

First Edition 10 9 8 7 6 5 4 3 2 1

Library of Congress Cataloging-in-Publication Data

Carle, Eric.

[Rooster who set out to see the world]

Rooster is off to see the world / by Eric Carle. — 1st ed.

p. cm. — (Ready-to-read)

Summary: A simple introduction to the meaning of numbers and sets as a rooster, on his way to see the world, is joined by fourteen animals along the way.

[1. Animals—Fiction. 2. Counting.] I. Title.

PZ7.C21476Ro 2013

[E]—dc23

2012017059

ISBN 978-1-4424-7269-3 (pbk)

ISBN 978-1-4424-7270-9 (hc)

This book was previously published with slightly different text as *Rooster's Off to See the World*.

One morning a rooster set

out to see the world.

He had not gone far

when he began to feel lonely.

Then the rooster met two cats.

"Come with me to see

the world," said the rooster.

"We would love to,"

said the cats.

So they set off

down the road.

Then the rooster and the

cats met three frogs.

"Would you like to see the

world?" asked the rooster.

"Why not?" said the frogs.

"We are not busy now."

So the frogs followed

the rooster and the cats.

Then the rooster, the cats,

and the frogs met

four turtles.

"Would you like to see the

world?" asked the rooster.

"It might be fun,"

snapped one of the turtles.

So they all set off

to see the world.

Then the rooster, the cats,
the frogs, and the turtles
saw five fish.

The fish asked
where they were going.

"We're off to see the world,"

said the rooster.

The fish wanted to join them,

so they all set off

to see the world.

Soon it got dark.

"Where is our dinner?"

asked the cats.

"Where do we sleep?"
asked the frogs.

"We are cold,"
said the turtles.

Fireflies flew up above.

"We are scared,"

said the fish.

The rooster did not

know what to say.

The fish wanted to go home,

so they swam away.

The turtles began to think

about their warm house.

They turned

and crawled back

down the road.

The frogs wanted

to go home too.

"Have a good evening,"

they said

as they jumped away

one by one.

The cats went home too.

"Have a good trip,"

they said.

Then the rooster

was all alone.

He had not seen the world.

The rooster looked
at the moon and said,
"I miss my home."

The moon did not answer.

It, too, went away.

The rooster turned

and went home.

He ate his grain and
happily sat on his perch.
Then he went to sleep.

The rooster had

a wonderful dream—

about a trip

around the world!